SHOVEL KNIGHT

DIGGER'S DIARY

by Gabe Soria
with the assistance of Caleb Soria

Grosset & Dunlap
An Imprint of Penguin Random House

GROSSET & DUNLAP
Penguin Young Readers Group
An Imprint of Penguin Random House LLC

YACHT CLUB
GAMES

Photo credits: p. 46: Brand X Pictures/Thinkstock.

ISBN 9781101996034

10 9 8 7 6 5 4 3 2 1

Shovel Knight wants YOU...

...to come along on an ADVENTURE!

This is the realm of Shovel Knight, a faraway land of valiant knights and noble creatures. But a shadow covers our valley, cast by the fearsome forces of the **ENCHANTRESS** and the **ORDER OF NO QUARTER**. With your heroic help, we will free the land of the evil enchantment. Let's dig in!

All adventures need a historian to chronicle what has happened, and indeed, that's what this diary is: YOUR chronicle of what's to come. And here to help you on this journey is the ballad-friendly Bard.

THIS DIGGER'S DIARY
IS THE CHRONICLE
OF THE KNIGHT
KNOWN AS . . .

[YOUR NAME HERE]

HARKEN YE TO THE
WORDS OF THE SCRIBE!

This is SHOVEL KNIGHT.
You know this. Why?

This helmet is famous throughout the land.

DESIGN A HELMET!

Use this space to design your own unique helmet. Strike fear into the hearts of the Order of No Quarter!

Here are some other well-known helmets.

Black Knight

King Knight

Polar Knight

Nice Moves!

Do you have any special moves like Shovel Knight's Shovel Drop? Name your special moves, then describe what they do.

SHOVEL DROP: Attack from the air by landing

on your opponent.

IF YOU'VE EVER READ AN ADVENTURE STORY, you've read the work of some scribes. List your favorite adventure stories below.

I PREFER THE STORY OF HOW THE ENCHANTRESS CONQUERED THE KNIGHTS OF THE VALLEY.

PRACTICE YOUR SCRIBING SKILLS

Write about an adventure you've had in *your* life.

I'VE HAD MANY A HARROWING HAT ADVENTURE! EVERY GOOD HAT HAS A TOP, A MIDDLE, AND A BOTTOM, AND A GOOD ADVENTURE HAS A BEGINNING, A MIDDLE, AND AN END.

I SING ABOUT VALIANT KNIGHTS AND EPIC ADVENTURES! MAKE YOURS WORTH A SONG!

Write dialogue for Shovel Knight that fits your story.

SHOVEL KNIGHT IS KNOWN THROUGHOUT THE LAND FOR HIS SUPERB SHOVEL SKILLS.

List your top five tools and toys here.

1 --

2 --

3 --

4 --

5 --

I PREFER POTIONS!

Now pick your **FAVORITE**. Got it? That's your new knight name! You're ⬚⬚⬚⬚⬚ Knight!

Okay, _____ Knight—what do you look like?

Draw yourself below.

DECIDEDLY DASHING!

THE CODES OF SHOVELRY: SLASH MERCILESSLY AND DIG TIRELESSLY!

Creed #1

- -

- -

Creed #2

- -

- -

Creed #3

- -

- -

A CREED IS A SAYING THAT SUMS UP WHAT YOU STAND FOR. THINK OF SOME CREEDS FOR YOURSELF. MAKE THEM CATCHY, JUST LIKE SHOVEL KNIGHT'S!

WHAT DO YOU BRING TO BATTLE?

Shovel Knight carries all he can to help in his adventures.

Fill in all the empty spaces below with pictures of stuff you think you'd need for an adventure. Don't be shy—the sky's the limit!

RELICS

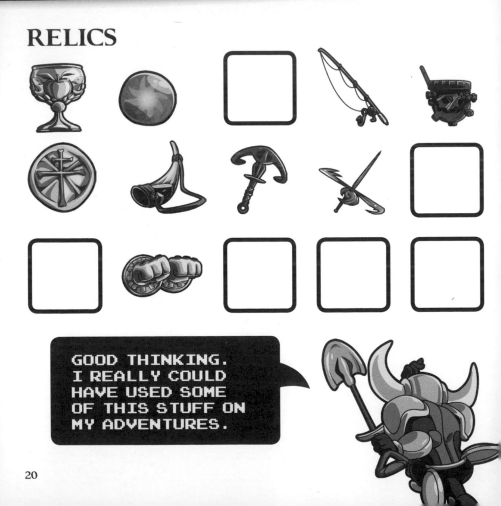

GOOD THINKING. I REALLY COULD HAVE USED SOME OF THIS STUFF ON MY ADVENTURES.

THE ORDER OF NO QUARTER

These knights are known for their villainy. Feel free to deface these posters with your own graffiti! Look, someone has already done it to King Knight's poster.

WANTED

King Knight

WANTED

Specter Knight

WANTED

Tinker Knight

WANTED

Treasure Knight

Deface these posters, too.

WANTED
Mole Knight

WANTED
Plague Knight

WANTED
Polar Knight

WANTED
Propeller Knight

THE VILE VILLAINS

(But do you dare deface *these* posters?!)

WELCOME, WEARY TRAVELER, TO THE VILLAGE, HOME TO FRIENDS, FOES, AND FOLKS IN BETWEEN. HERE, GOLD IS THE

ONLY KING, AND YOU CAN EARN AND
SPEND AN ENTIRE FORTUNE IF YOU
LOOK IN THE RIGHT PLACES.

HALT, TRAVELER! FARRELS IS DEMANDING THAT YOU GIVE UP YOUR WEAPON BEFORE ENTERING THE VILLAGE. BEHOLD THE WEAPONS, ITEMS, AND CONTRABAND HE HAS CONFISCATED.

Draw the weapons in Farrels's arsenal.

THE VILLAGERS ARE NOBLE AND PROUD. DRAW YOUR OWN VILLAGERS BELOW.

The Bard lost his music sheets, and they have been spread across the land. Shovel Knight heroically returns the ballads here for gold and a song.

A BALLAD IS A POEM OR A SONG THAT TELLS A STORY.

THERE ONCE WAS A KNIGHT WITH A PLAN; HE SEARCHED FOR HIS FRIEND 'CROSS THE LAND. HE FOUGHT WITH HIS BLADE, AT THE SIDE OF HIS MAID, AND HIS QUEST WAS NOBLE AND GRAND.

Write your heroic ballad on the scroll on the next page.

Song title: _ _ _ _ _ _ _ _ _ _ _ _ _ _ _

Performer: _ _ _ _ _ _ _ _ _ _ _ _ _ _ _

Description: _ _ _ _ _ _ _ _ _ _ _ _ _

_ _

_ _

_ _

_ _

_ _

_ _

Upon finishing your beautiful ballad, sing out! Fill the halls of your home with song until you are joined by your familial throng. **TIP: TRY SINGING TO A TUNE YOU KNOW (I.E., "ROW ROW ROW YOUR BOAT").**

THAT WAS GREAT!
TRY WRITING TWO MORE SONGS.

Song title: _ _ _ _ _ _ _ _ _ _ _ _ _ _

Performer: _ _ _ _ _ _ _ _ _ _ _ _ _ _

Description: _ _ _ _ _ _ _ _ _ _ _ _

_ _ _ _ _ _ _ _ _ _ _ _ _ _ _ _ _ _ _ _

Song title: _ _ _ _ _ _ _ _ _ _ _ _ _

Performer: _ _ _ _ _ _ _ _ _ _ _ _ _

Description: _ _ _ _ _ _ _ _ _ _ _

_ _

_ _

_ _

_ _

_ _

_ _

_ _

_ _

_ _

_ _

WHAT ARE THE BEST SONGS YOU'VE EVER HEARD? LIST THEM BELOW WITH DUTIFUL DETAIL OF THEIR BEAUTY.

HAVE I GOT A
DEAL FOR YOU!

Chester wheels and deals and always has some useful relics to sell that will help Shovel Knight defeat evil. If you were like Chester and decided to sell your favorite objects, what would you sell and how much would you charge for each item? Draw them here and list their prices!

Grandma Swamp isn't a witch, but she resembles one! Draw your best witch here. Make sure the witch says something that sounds like Latin, such as **"EXCAVATIO!"** like Grandma Swamp would say. Witchy, indeed!

I SAID I'M
NOT A WITCH!

WORD SEARCH

Find these characters hidden in the block of letters!

Croaker
King Knight
Shield Knight
The Enchantress

Polar Knight
Mona
Troupple King
Percy

Reize
Goatician

```
P Y M T X V I R D K K D D V S
O C A H R Y Y P E I H B L S W
L R M U M O N A N K K M E M S
A E M G J R U G U R A R F Y Y
R P S S Q K K P V E T O F B C
K T O B Z N T Z P N W V R O R
N Q D J I I R P A L P B K C T
I E K G K T H H A T E G K Y M
G W H K V P C N Z T Y K G N A
H T T I X N G C J Y S Z I X W
T S H I E L D K N I G H T N E
C L A E N A I C I T A O G Z G
G W H T T R G V R N C F I X T
T T Q W O M C A V Z E E G C J
L G Q C K H C I H B R Q N O Y
```

During his journey, Shovel Knight finds a host of secret passages that lead to treasure, relics, and music sheets. If you had a secret passage to anywhere you wanted to go, where would it lead? Make a list of cool secret passage ideas on this page and draw what they might look like on the next.

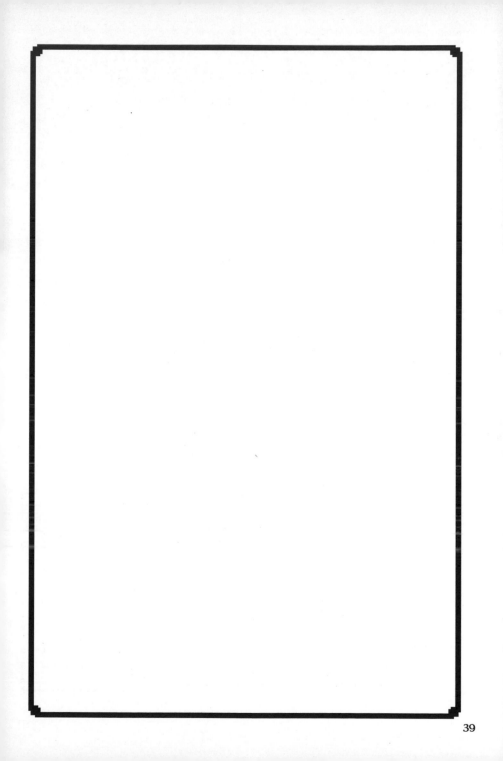

You have faced many foes, but **sometimes the biggest foe is the place itself, much like the Hall of Champions.** One can easily get lost. If Shovel Knight were trapped in a maze, could you assist him with his exit?

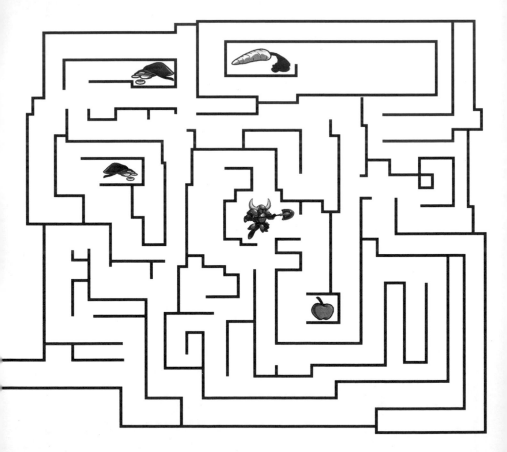

Shovel Knight finds lots of treasures on his quest, like colorful gems, gold coins, magic bottles, and food. What sort of treasure would *you* like to find? Draw it!

Why stop there?
Draw MORE TREASURE!
You're rich!

FEATS!

Feats are epic deeds. What feats have you accomplished? (Examples: getting good grades, learning to play sports.) Create icons for yourself that honor the work you've done.

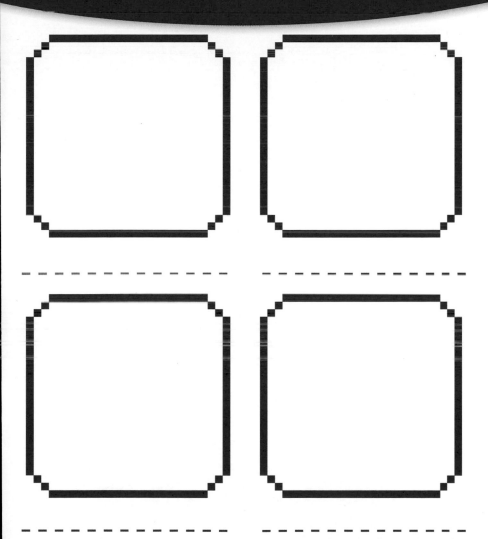

Ichors are magic potions that Shovel Knight gets from the Troupple King, and if he drinks them, he gets special powers. Now name your ichors. Make them WEIRD. And draw something mysterious coming out of the tops of the chalices while you're at it.

#1 - - - - - - - - - - - - - - -

#2 - - - - - - - - - - - - - -

#3 - - - - - - - - - - - - - -

#4 - - - - - - - - - - - - -

#5 - - - - - - - - - - - - - -

THAT'S PRONOUNCED EYE-CORE!

Now describe your ichors.

What powers would they give you?

#1

#2

#3

#4

#5

Congratulations!

YOU'RE A TROUPPLE ACOLYTE, A FOLLOWER OF THE TROUPPLE KING AND HIS GREAT WORK TO AID THE HEROES OF THE LAND!

The Grizzled Seer often has advice to lend to Shovel Knight. For example, "Look before you leap!" Leave some advice for a future adventurer.

Shovel Knight is quite accomplished at discovering secrets.

Write some of your secrets here (don't worry, we won't tell).

Shovel Knight gets his energy back by eating chicken and apples. What would you want to eat while on an adventure? Draw all the goodies you would like below.

WRITE YOUR OWN MEAL TICKETS AND BE A GASTRONOMER!

The Gastronomer makes delicious food to give Shovel Knight more health. Why not come up with your own recipe for an adventuring snack? Think of something you could make and carry with you on a dangerous journey, like granola or a fruit snack, and write down the recipe on the meal ticket on the next page. Cookies, trail mix . . . anything that helps give a knight an edge!

NOW COME UP WITH YOUR OWN RECIPE.

Meal Ticket

SOUNDS DELICIOUS!

CREATE YOUR OWN MINIONS!

Each knight in the Order of No Quarter has minions that Shovel Knight must defeat as he battles his way through the level. Draw the minions that you encounter and defeat on your quest.

Beeto

Blorb

Birder

FOOLISH READER, YOU'VE CROSSED MY PATH. PREPARE TO HAVE YOUR ESSENCE TAKEN FROM YOU! I'LL SHOW YOU WHAT REAL FUN'S ALL ABOUT! HEE HEE HEE HEE!

BEGONE FROM THESE PAGES, PLAGUE KNIGHT! YOUR TREACHERY IS NOT WELCOME HERE.
CURSES! MY POTIONS FAILED ME NOW, BUT TRUST ME, FRIEND. I SHALL RETURN! HEE HEE HEE!

Shovel Knight isn't speechless,
he's just waiting for you to write him a line.
Make it something celebratory, like "For Shovelry!"

REMAKE THE WORLD OF SHOVEL KNIGHT THE WAY YOU WANT TO AND DRAW NEW LOCATIONS.

MAP LEGEND

Draw your new locations in the boxes and describe them so future travelers will know what they're getting into.

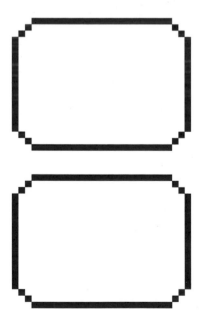

_____

_____

_____

_____

_____

_____

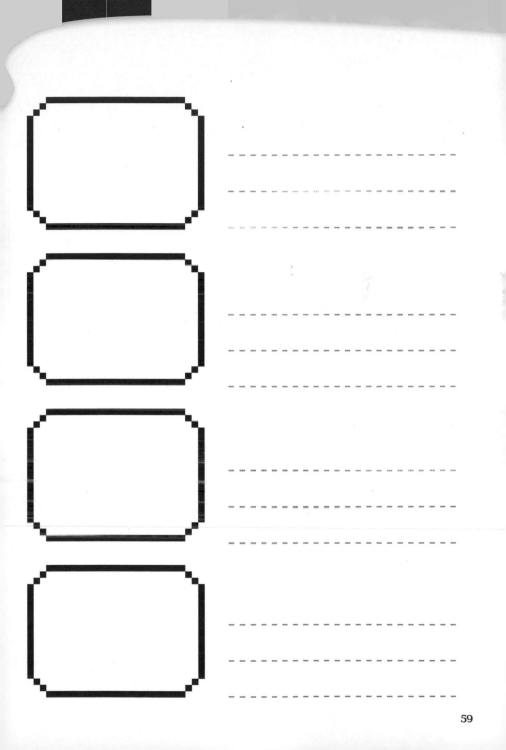

DRAW YOUR NEW LOCATIONS IN A CHALLENGING NEW ORDER.

WELCOME TO THE VALLEY. IF YOU WERE TO HELP ME CREATE NEW ADVENTURES, WHAT WOULD YOU CREATE?

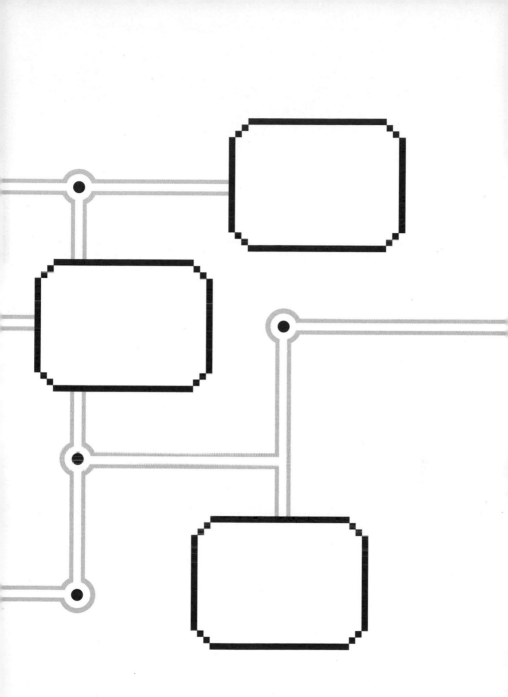

Answer these five trivia questions about the different lairs of the Order of No Quarter.

1. **As Shovel Knight advances toward the Tower of Fate, he must defeat Tinker Knight in his lair, known as:**

   a. The Clockwork Tower

   b. The Grandfather Clock Grotto

   c. The Vaulted Timepiece

   d. The Setting Sun Dial

2. **Polar Knight is an Order of No Quarter knight who serves the Enchantress. What is the name of his lair?**

   a. The Barren Boat

   b. The Stranded Ship

   c. The Capsized Canoe

   d. The Topsy-Turvy Tanker

3. What underwater lair is home to the evil Treasure Knight?

a. The Tin Tuna

b. The Copper Dolphin

c. The Iron Whale

d. The Rusty Manatee

4. Plague Knight resides in the volatile lair known as:

a. The Village

b. The Blast Factory

c. The Explodatorium

d. The Science Experiment

5. This lava-filled lair is home to Mole Knight:

a. The Missing Metropolis

b. The Found Village

c. The Forgotten Grotto

d. The Lost City

WATCH OUT!

Shovel Knight is facing off against a never-before-seen creature. It's so hideous, we couldn't bear to put its picture here. But that doesn't mean YOU can't draw it . . .

Sometimes, Shovel Knight uses a fishing rod to grab goodies.

Draw what's on the line today.

Describe what these travelers are doing. When you are wandering, where do you go? What do you do there? (You don't have to look for trouble.)

Reize   Phantom Striker   Mr. Hat   Baz

Shield Knight is Shovel Knight's dearest friend and companion.

Who is your closest adventure partner or friend? Do they have a special ability? Explain what makes them special here, and draw them on the next page.

Describe your friend.

- -

- -

- -

- -

- -

- -

- -

- -

- -

- - - - - - - - - - - - - - - - - - -

Draw your friend as a knight.

Draw you and your friend on an adventure with Shovel Knight!

MORE ADVENTURE!

The story of Shovel Knight doesn't have to end here. Write about his next great adventure on these conveniently blank scrolls.

CHAPTER 1
The Adventure Begins

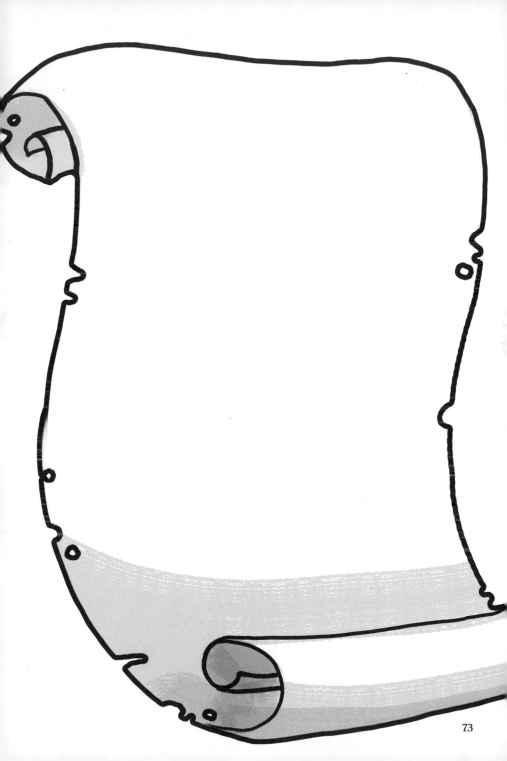

CHAPTER 2
The First Trial

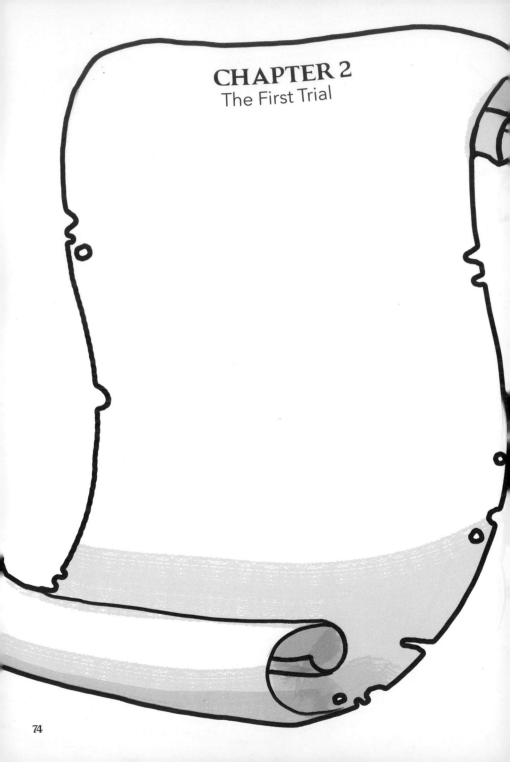

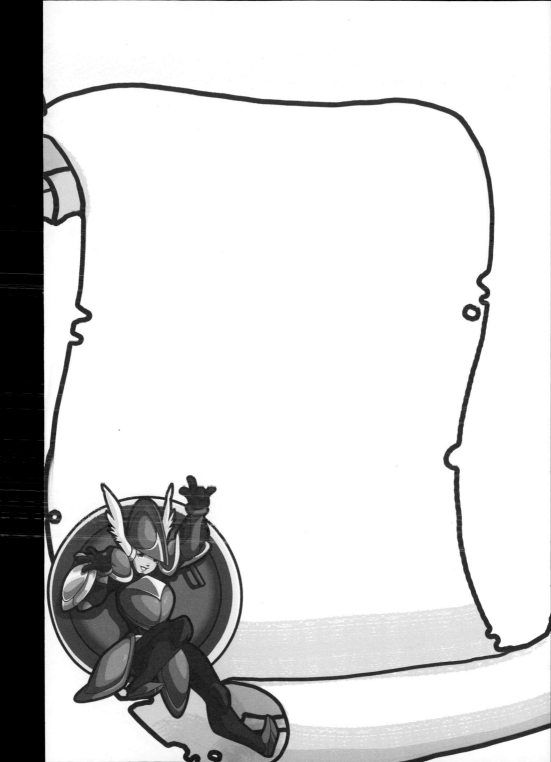

CHAPTER 3
The Second Trial

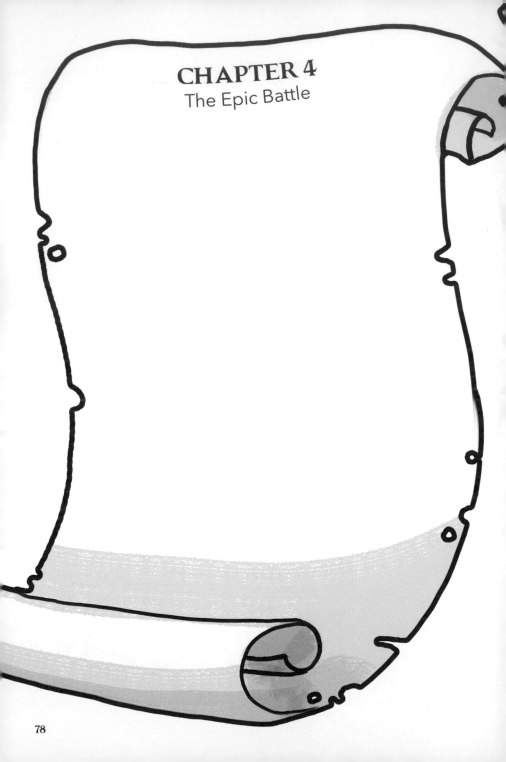

CHAPTER 4
The Epic Battle

CHAPTER 5
The Celebration

-THE END-

HEE HEE HEE! HAVING FUN WITH YOUR LITTLE ADVENTURE? I WONDER IF YOU WILL FARE BETTER BY JOINING US, THE ORDER OF NO QUARTER.

THE ORDER OF NO QUARTER
NEEDS NEW MEMBERS.
MISERY LOVES COMPANY,
SO IF YOU WANT TO
JOIN US, DRAW YOUR
VILLAINOUS SELF ON THE
RIGHT. DON'T FORGET
YOUR EVIL KNIGHT NAME!

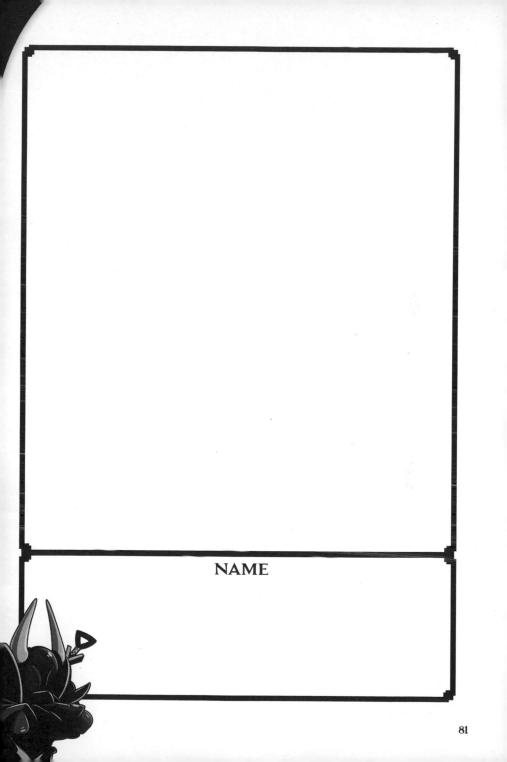

NAME

Now that you've created your own villainous knight, draw two more new knights to join our ranks and name them.

NAME

NAME

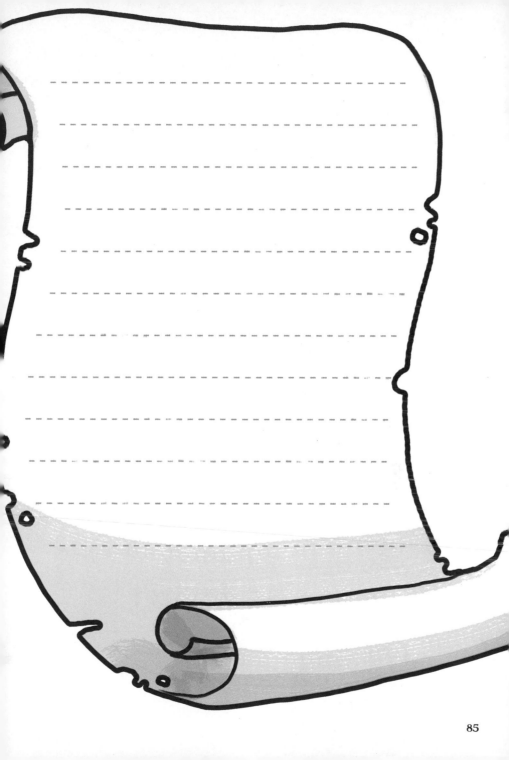

Every member of the Order of No Quarter gets their own evil lair to hang out in. What's YOURS called? What's the theme of the lair and how does that represent your evil knight? Write it in the box below in scary letters.

OOH! HOW DEVIOUS!
HEE HEE HEE!
COMING UP WITH
A NAME IS ONE
THING . . .

. . . CREATING YOUR LAIR IS ANOTHER! DOES IT HAVE SPECIFIC TRAPS AND HAZARDS, LIKE THE SLIPPERY, FROZEN SURFACES OF POLAR KNIGHT'S LAIR, OR CASCADING RIVERS OF FIRE, LIKE MOLE KNIGHT'S LAIR? DESCRIBE IT IN EVIL DETAIL BELOW.

MONSTERS

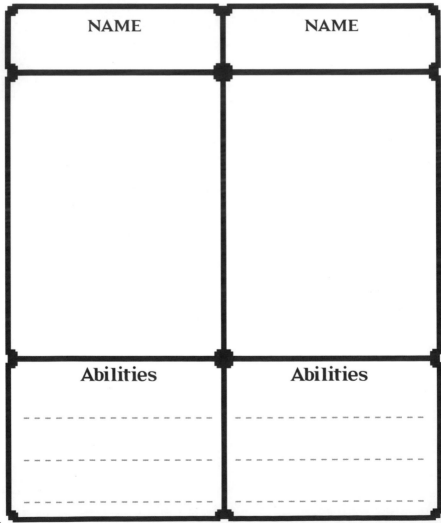

NAME

NAME

Abilities

Abilities

What's a lair without monsters? Create some fearsome foes to fight do-gooder knights. Give your monsters a name and describe their abilities.

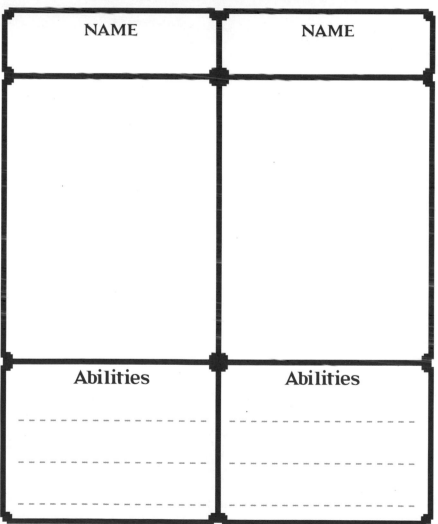

NAME	NAME
Abilities	**Abilities**

Every knight in the Order of No Quarter needs some lackeys in their lair to do their bidding. Using the magic of your pen, turn these squiggles into creeps and beasts! Use the monsters surrounding these pages for inspiration.

Blorb

Goldarmor

Boneclang

Hoverhaft Moler Propeller Rat

Every great creature has to have a great name. Think of some names for the creatures you just created.

Here's a hint: Use stuff around you for inspiration—strange objects, and even your friends and family! Combine words (such as Blitz and Steed into Blitzsteed) to make your names distinctive.

Floatsome　　　**Beeto**

. . . CAN YOU CREATE AN EVEN BIGGER MINIBOSS FOR YOUR OWN LAIR? I BET YOU CAN'T! DRAW SHOVEL KNIGHT IN ACTION TRYING TO DEFEAT YOUR CREATION.

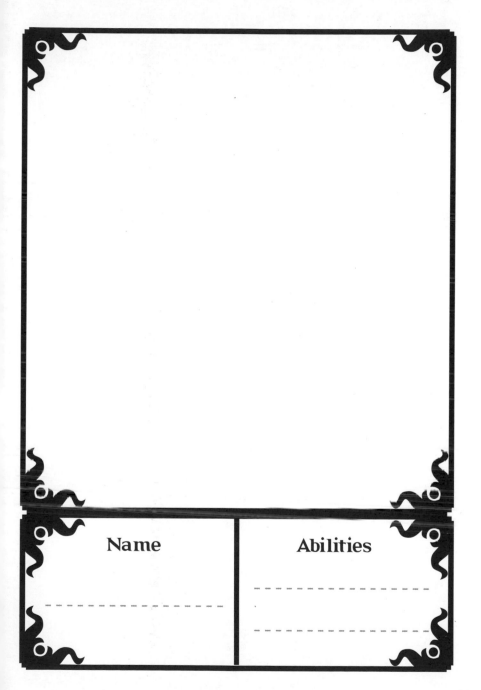

Name

Abilities

SKULL SKILLS

Boneclangs are some of the best flunkies to have on your side. Fill the next two pages with drawings of skulls and skeletons to create your own skeleton army!

WHO'S THE BOSS?

It happens to the bravest of knights:
SHOVEL KNIGHT has made it all the way through your evil lair and is trying to defeat you. Show him your stuff!

YOU ARE!

Draw your villainous knight giving a special attack as you try to defeat Shovel Knight.

CONGRATULATIONS, FAIR KNIGHT. YOUR EVIL IS TO BE COMMENDED. I MUST HAVE YOU JOIN THE ORDER OF NO QUARTER OFFICIALLY.

NEFARIOUS PLOTS
AND SCHEMES

Use these blank pages to write down and draw some of your ideas for bad stuff to do to heroic knights. Draw your various villainous knights battling Shovel Knight and describe the action.

OR USE IT FOR WHATEVER YOU WANT—NO ONE TELLS US EVIL KNIGHTS WHAT TO DO!

Shovel Knight draws his Shovel Blade. How will you attack?

**Shovel Knight uses the Shovel Drop.
How will you get out of the way?**

Shovel Knight is charging. What will you do?

Imagine if this book were a video game and you had the opportunity to go back to the start and change things, from the challenges to the activities.

Go back to your favorite and least favorite pages and rewrite this book. Give yourself new challenges and complete them in whatever space you have left!

Thanks
for reading!